Goodnight, Sleepyville

illustrated by

Blake Liliane Hellman • **Steven Henry**

BLOOMSBURY
CHILDREN'S BOOKS

NEW YORK LONDON OXFORD NEW DELHI SYDNEY

BLOOMSBURY CHILDREN'S BOOKS
Bloomsbury Publishing Inc., part of Bloomsbury Publishing Plc
1385 Broadway, New York, NY 10018

BLOOMSBURY, BLOOMSBURY CHILDREN'S BOOKS, and the Diana logo are trademarks of Bloomsbury Publishing Plc

First published in the United States of America in June 2020
by Bloomsbury Children's Books

Bloomsbury books may be purchased for business or promotional use. For information on bulk
purchases please contact Macmillan Corporate and Premium Sales Department at
specialmarkets@macmillan.com

Library of Congress Cataloging-in-Publication Data
Names: Hellman, Blake Liliane, author. | Henry, Steven, illustrator.
Title: Goodnight, Sleepyville / by Blake Liliane Hellman ; illustrated by Steven Henry.
Description: New York : Bloomsbury Children's Books, 2020.
Summary: While the sun goes down in Sleepyville, animals of all kinds are choosing pajamas, snuggling into bed, and enjoying a
lullaby or story as they look forward to sweet dreams.
Identifiers: LCCN 2019044644 (print) | LCCN 2019044645 (e-book)
ISBN 978-1-68119-876-7 (hardcover) • ISBN 978-1-68119-877-4 (e-book) • ISBN 978-1-68119-878-1 (e-PDF)
Subjects: CYAC: Bedtime—Fiction. | Animals—Fiction.
Classification: LCC PZ7.1.H4468 Goo 2020 (print) | LCC PZ7.1.H4468 (e-book) | DDC [E]—dc23
LC record available at https://lccn.loc.gov/2019044644

Art created with pencil, watercolor, and gouache
Typeset in Century Storybook
Book design by Jeanette Levy
Printed in China by RR Donnelley, Dongguan City, Guangdong
2 4 6 8 10 9 7 5 3 1

All papers used by Bloomsbury Publishing Plc are natural, recyclable products made from wood grown in well-managed forests.
The manufacturing processes conform to the environmental regulations of the country of origin.

To find out more about our authors and books
visit www.bloomsbury.com and sign up for our newsletters.

For Wini
—B. L. H. & S. H.

In Sleepyville,
the sun is setting,
and everyone's
done for the day.

Sweeping,

shutting,

strutting.

To simple homes,

dome-homes,

teensy-
weensy
homes,

. . . and very fancy homes.

Hang up your hat,

slip off your shoes,

and wash your
paws for supper.

Then after the dishes are done,

it's time for milk and cookies.

Put on your favorite pajamas.

Stripes,

plaid,

or polka-dots?

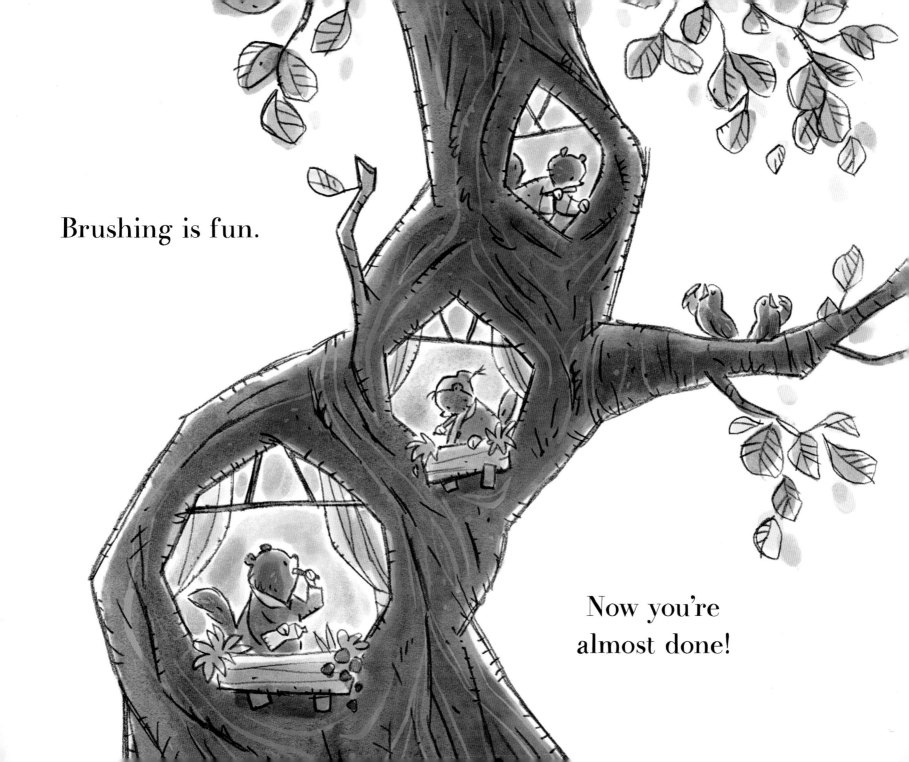

Brushing is fun.

Now you're
almost done!

Let's snuggle,

wiggle,

cuddle.

In Sleepyville, down goes the sun,

and up comes the moon.

Though some
are tucked in,
snug as a bug . . .

. . . others need a lullaby.

And maybe a
bedtime story.

Some drift,

some curl,

some sink
into dreams.

And if you look up,
you can see the stars
twinkling in the sky.

Goodnight, Sleepyville.

All the lights go out . . .

. . . except one.